FRIENDS
OF ACPL

*With huge appreciation*
*for the "Honest" family*
*(sometimes known as Clark)*
*J. B.*

*To Mum and Dad*
*L. C.*

A Doubleday Book for Young Readers

Published by Random House Children's Books
a division of Random House, Inc., 1540 Broadway, New York, New York 10036

Doubleday and the anchor with dolphin colophon are registered trademarks of Random House, Inc.

Text copyright © 2000 by Jemma Beeke
Illustrations copyright © 2000 by Lynne Chapman

First American Edition 2001
First Published in Great Britain in 2000 by David & Charles Children's Books

Visit us on the Web! www. randomhouse.com/kids
Educators and librarians, for a variety of teaching tools, visit us at
www.randomhouse.com/teachers

Library of Congress Cataloging-in-Publication Data
ISBN: 0-385-32795-1
Cataloging-in-Publication Data is available from the Library of Congress.

February 2001

10 9 8 7 6 5 4 3 2 1

# The
# RICKETY BARN
# SHOW

Written by Jemma Beeke
Illustrated by Lynne Chapman

A Doubleday Book for Young Readers

All was quiet at Rickety Barn Farm. The animals
were lazily chewing grass or snoozing in the sunshine.
It looked like just another ordinary day.

Jasper the cat was lapping his morning milk
when a wonderful plan popped into his head.

"I'll put on a show!" he thought.

He made a huge poster to
pin on the door of the Rickety Barn.
"There!" he said to himself. "All the other
animals will love my performance."

Jasper thought he had better
start practicing right away.

Rickety Barn
SHOW
today
at 3 o'clock
(everybody
welcome)
Miiiaaooow!
Miiaaoo w!
Miiaaoow!

"Why are you singing?" asked Sniggle the pig as he passed by. Jasper whispered in his ear, "I'm getting ready for the show."

**"Show? What show?"** squealed Sniggle loudly.
"Shhh! The Rickety Barn Show, of course," Jasper replied grandly.
"How exciting," said Sniggle. "Might a pig be in it too?"

Jasper wanted to be the star of his show,
but he didn't want to disappoint his friend.
"Well . . . what can you do?" he asked.
"Accompany your singing with a one-pig band,"
announced Sniggle, and he trotted off to practice.

"Why are you toot-tooting on that bugle?" asked Suzie the hen.

"I'm getting ready for the show," Sniggle whispered.

**"Show? What show?"** clucked Suzie in excitement.

"The Rickety Barn Show, what else!" declared Sniggle.

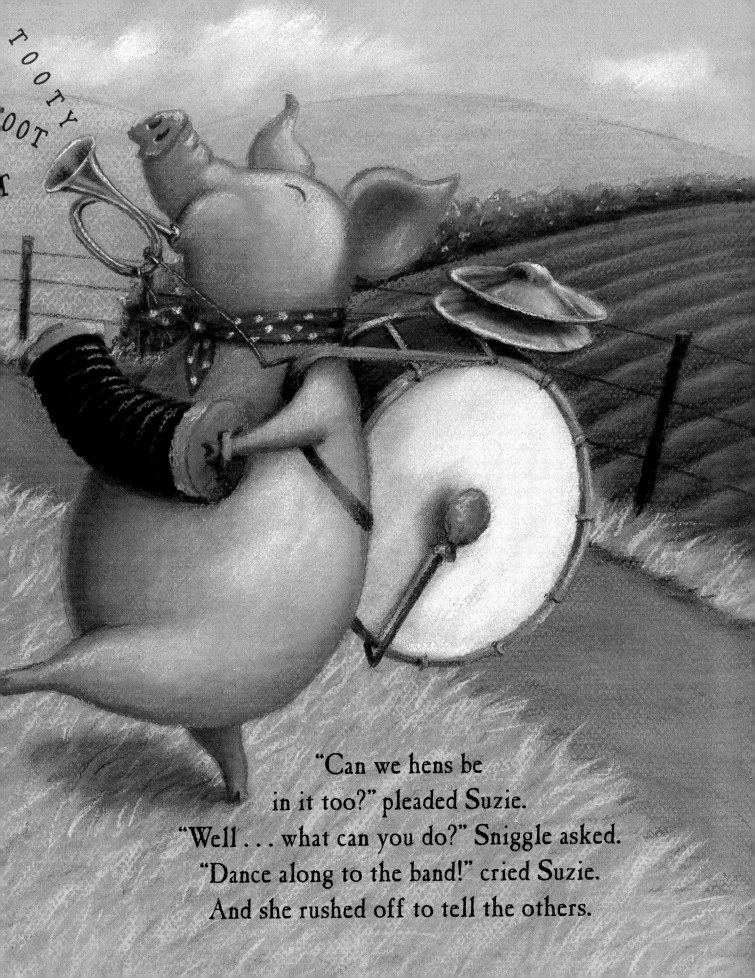

"Can we hens be
in it too?" pleaded Suzie.
"Well . . . what can you do?" Sniggle asked.
"Dance along to the band!" cried Suzie.
And she rushed off to tell the others.

"What's all this rowdy nonsense?"
Austin the old cart horse asked bossily.

"We're getting ready for the show," bragged Suzie.

**"Show? What show?"** Austin asked
with a rare whinny of excitement.

"The Rickety Barn Show, of course!"
chorused the hens joyfully.

"Sounds delightful," said Austin.
"I'd like to offer my services."
"Well . . . what can you do?" Suzie asked Austin.
"Bring an air of dignity to the proceedings," he announced.
"I will be reciting a short poem that I will make up specially."
And he plodded off to practice.

Flora the sheep appeared.

"Great poem, Austin! But why are you reciting it to yourself?" Flora asked.

Austin looked around with a superior air.

"I'm getting ready for the show," he declared.

**"Show? What show?"** bleated Flora loudly.

Oh littl
upo

La-dee-dah!

TOOT!
TOOT!
TOOT!

♪ ♫
Miiaaoow!

flower
the ground...

"The Rickety Barn Show, of course," replied Austin stuffily.
"How maaaaarvelous. Can we sheep be in it too?" pleaded Flora.
"Well . . ." Austin pondered. "What can you do?"
"An acrobatics display," announced Flora
as she skipped away to tell the others.

"Yoo-hoo! What's happening?"
mooed Chloe the cow.
"We're getting ready for the show!"
called Flora from the top of
the swaying pyramid.

**"Show? What show?"**
asked Chloe.

"Haven't you heard? The Rickety Ba-aarn Show!"
replied all the sheep together.
"Oooo, what fun! Can the cows be in it too?" pleaded Chloe.
"Ma-a-aybe . . . what can you do?" Flora asked.
"Perform a juggling act," boasted Chloe,
and she hurried off to tell the others.

Just before three o'clock, all the performers gathered in the Rickety Barn. Bruce stood by the door to welcome the audience, and the other animals huddled nervously behind the hay bales.

At three o'clock,
nobody had arrived
to watch the show.

By five past three,
the animals were starting
to shuffle their feet.

By ten past three,
still nobody had come
through the door
of the Rickety Barn.

"Where is everyone?" muttered Jasper.
"I've no idea!" replied Austin grumpily.
Then Sniggle squealed with laughter.

The others gave him a puzzled look.
"There's nobody to watch the show,"
he laughed, "because . . .

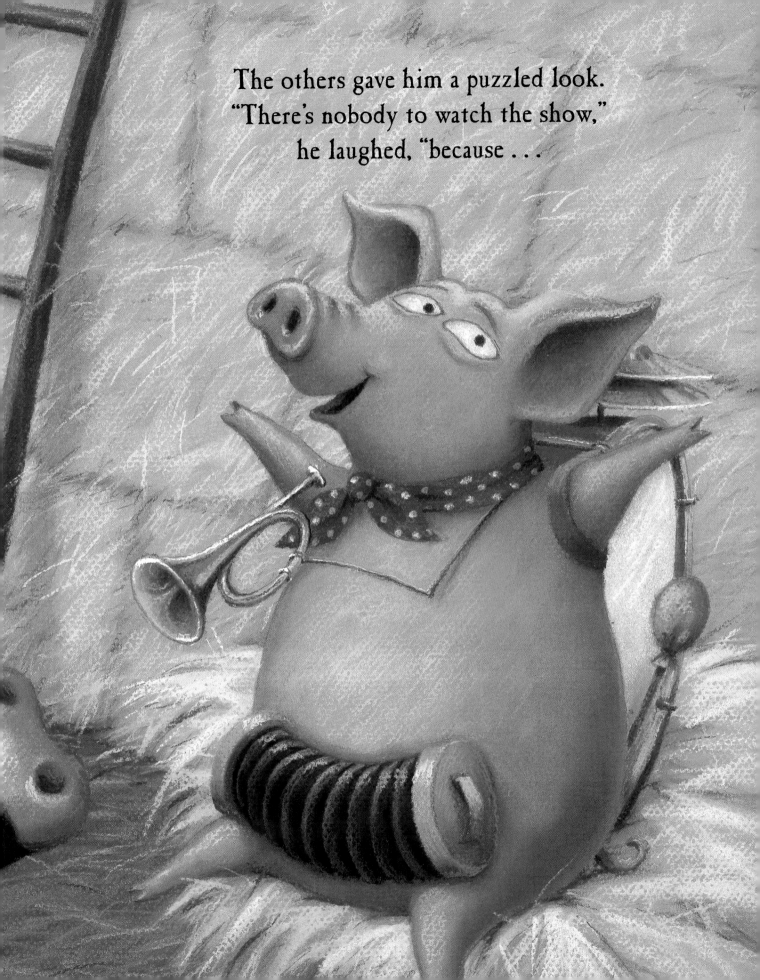

. . .we're all in it!"
There was only one thing to do.
"The show must go on!"
cried Jasper.
And it did.